SURVIVAL GUIDE TO

Written and Illustrated by Scoular Anderson

Collins
An Imprint of HarperCollinsPublishers

Also by Scoular Anderson

Survival Guide to Parents
Survival Guide to Pets

And by Brough Girling and Judy Brown

Survival Guide to School
Survival Guide to Friends
Survival Guide to Parties

First published in Great Britain by Collins in 1996
Collins is an imprint of
HarperCollins*Publishers* Ltd.,
77 - 85 Fulham Palace Road,
Hammersmith, London W6 8JB

1 3 5 7 9 8 6 4 2

Copyright © Scoular Anderson 1996

ISBN 0 00 675110 5

The author asserts the moral right to be
identified as the author of the work.

Printed and bound in Great Britain
by HarperCollins Manufacturing Ltd., Glasgow.

Conditions of Sale
This book is sold subject to the condition that it shall not by
way of trade or otherwise, be lent, re-sold, hired out or
otherwise circulated without the publisher's prior consent in
any form of binding or cover other than that in which it is
published and without a similar condition including this
condition being imposed on the subsequent purchaser.

MENU

Artistic Food	8
Breakfast Food	12
Call Me Parsley	16
Dodgy Food	20
Electronic Food	24
F.A.S.T. Food and F.A.R.T.S. Food	30
Green Food	35
Hot Food	40
Identifying Food	46
Joke Food	52
The Kitchen	55
Lunchbox Food	60
Missile Food	66
Night Food	68
Odorous Food	70
Party Food	73
Quirky Food	75
Record-breaking Food	78
Secret Food	80
Tummy-gurgling Food	82
Useful Food	83
Vanishing Food	85
Weather Forecasting with Food	86
X-Rated Food	89
Youngster Food	92
Zombie Food	96

WELCOME

...to the Food Research Institute for Experimentation and Development, known as **F.R.I.E.D.**

We hope this little visit will help you to survive food. The main problem of surviving food is that you need food to survive. You and food are going to have to get along with each other whether you like it or not.

"Amanda, finish your meal!"

"I can't. I want to send it to F.R.I.E.D. The cabbage is the limpest cabbage in the world. The smell has just killed two flies stone-dead and the sausages have done twenty press-ups each."

Here is the director of F.R.I.E.D., Professor Irma Itsgonoff, to say a few words...

So now let's have a look inside some of F.R.I.E.D.'s laboratories...

LABORATORY A
ARTISTIC FOOD

You can survive some foods by using them in a creative way. Have a look at Laboratory A's gallery for one or two ideas.

Fruit and vegetables make excellent decorations for snowmen and snowomen.

Potatoes are very versatile. Sculptures can be made with mashed potatoes (plus a little mayonnaise and seasoning).

You can create smart, chunky jewellery by stringing potatoes together. (Remember to scrub them first.)

Soft, mushy things can be used instead of paint. You simply throw the items at the canvas to create a colourful abstract.

If you use a very big piece of bread instead of a canvas, the picture can be sprinkled with cheese and lightly grilled for supper.

LABORATORY B
BREAKFAST FOOD

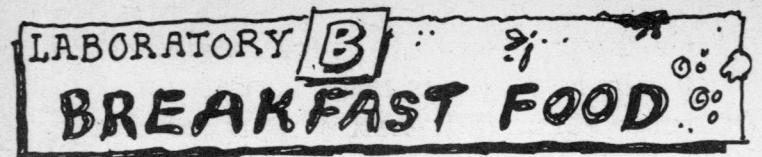

At breakfast you eat the first food of the day. There are two problems with breakfast.

PROBLEM 1 – You're asleep

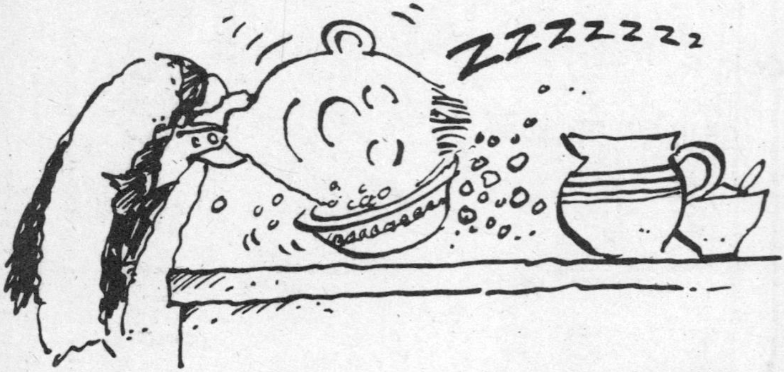

PROBLEM 2 – Breakfast cereals

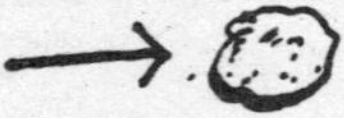

Let's face it, these tiddly bits of dried crinkly stuff are not the most exciting foods to meet first thing in the morning.

Cereals come in all shapes and sizes. Kevin Parsley has been saving cereals for years and here's part of his collection.

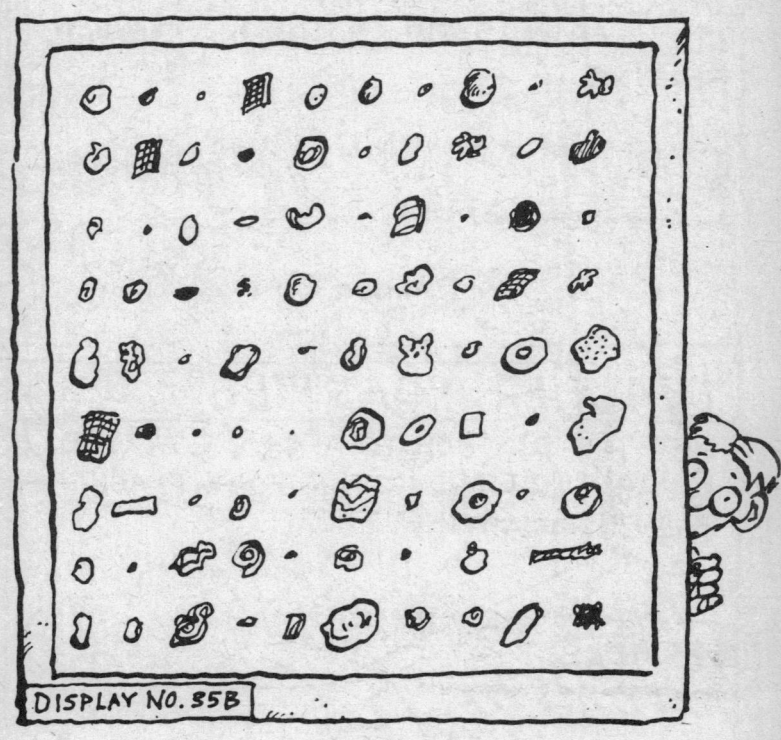

DISPLAY NO. 35B

However, to help you survive breakfasts, the scientists in Laboratory B have developed some exciting new cereals...

CRACKLING CRUNCHIES

THESE ARE THE FIREWORKS OF THE CEREAL WORLD. GOOD FOR WAKING YOU UP. JUST ADD MILK AND WATCH THEM GO. KEEP PETS OUT OF THE ROOM WHEN SERVING.

TEACHER TOASTIES

GET THE DAY OFF TO A GOOD START BY POURING HOT MILK OVER YOUR <u>TEACHERS</u>, THEN SWALLOWING THEM.

FLOATERS

MULTI-FLAVOURED FLOATERS ALLOW YOU TO EXERCISE WHILE EATING YOUR BREAKFAST. FLOATERS FLOAT UPWARDS WHEN POURED FROM THE PACKET. USE A STEPLADDER RATHER THAN A BOWL — TREMENDOUS FUN.

GRUNCHIE GIFTS

FOR THOSE WHO PREFER THE FREE GIFTS INSIDE CEREAL PACKETS, HERE'S A PACKET FULL OF GIFTS WITH ONE FREE CEREAL. YOU'LL BE HUNGRY BUT NOT BORED.

LABORATORY C
CALL ME PARSLEY

Some people are named after foods - Kevin Parsley for one. If you get teased for having a foodish name, you can survive this by remembering the famous people who sounded edible.

Laboratory C spends its time searching for famous foody folk, like:

ATTILA THE BUN

FAMOUS WARRIOR-GENERAL WHO PILLAGED HIS WAY ROUND EUROPE.

KEVIN PARSLEY

FAMOUS ... ER ...

LUDWIG VAN BEETROOT

FAMOUS COMPOSER WHO WENT DEAF.

SIR FRANCIS CAKE

FAMOUS ELIZABETHAN SEAMAN WHO DEFEATED THE SPANISH ARMADA.

JULIUS CHEESER

FAMOUS ROMAN GENERAL AND EMPEROR.

ALEXANDRE TRIFLE

FAMOUS FRENCH ENGINEER WHO BUILT THE TRIFLE TOWER IN PARIS.

LABORATORY D
DODGY FOOD

There are two kinds of Dodgy Foods - poisonous food and poisoned food. Many toadstools are poisonous and you might not survive them if you go on a toadstool binge.

Some people put poison in food to give whoever eats it a nasty turn. Remember what happened to poor old Snow White when she took a bite of a dodgy apple - she dozed off for a year or two. Of course, you may see this as an advantage - you'd miss a lot of school and tonnes of homework.

Some poisoned foods can be more deadly. May we bring to your attention King Stanislav the Weak? His wife Gertrude killed him with a poisoned cake.

Queen Gertrude never was much of a baker.

Many kings employed royal tasters to taste their food and thus avoid a poisoning accident. If *you* are worried about being poisoned, you could get members of your family to taste things but you'd probably end up with a lot of fat brothers and sisters, cats and dogs.

Laboratory D has come up with a five-point plan for checking for poisoned food. Your family may not like this but it's better to be SAFE THAN SORRY!!

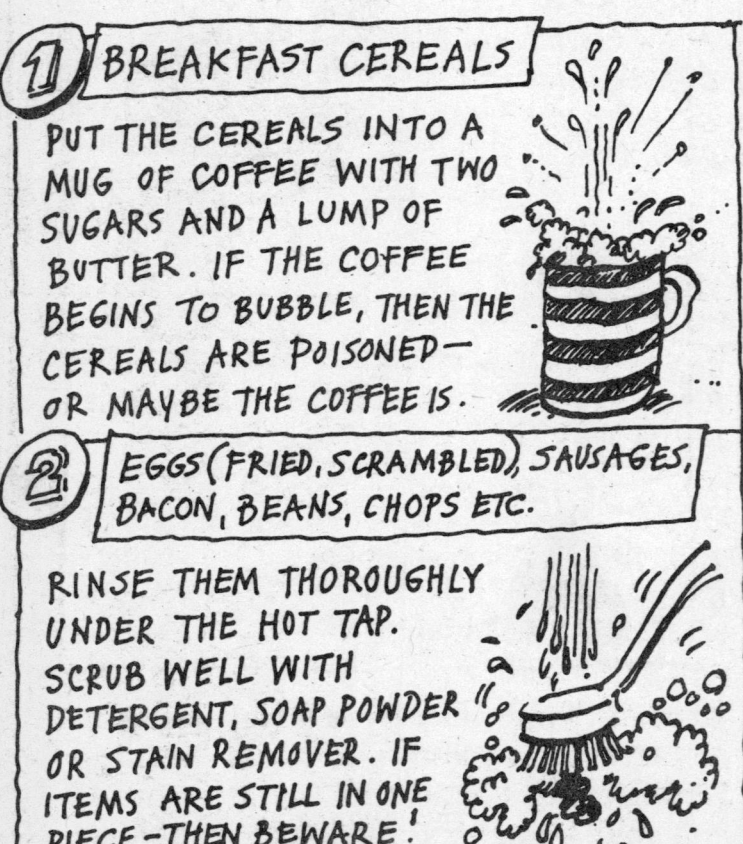

1) BREAKFAST CEREALS

PUT THE CEREALS INTO A MUG OF COFFEE WITH TWO SUGARS AND A LUMP OF BUTTER. IF THE COFFEE BEGINS TO BUBBLE, THEN THE CEREALS ARE POISONED — OR MAYBE THE COFFEE IS.

2) EGGS (FRIED, SCRAMBLED), SAUSAGES, BACON, BEANS, CHOPS ETC.

RINSE THEM THOROUGHLY UNDER THE HOT TAP. SCRUB WELL WITH DETERGENT, SOAP POWDER OR STAIN REMOVER. IF ITEMS ARE STILL IN ONE PIECE — THEN <u>BEWARE</u>! THEY'RE POISONED.

3) TOAST, BREAD, BISCUITS, CAKE

BREAK THEM INTO TINY LITTLE BITS THEN EXAMINE THEM CLOSELY WITH A MAGNIFYING GLASS. LITTLE, BRIGHTLY-COLOURED BITS COULD MEAN _POISON_. OR PERHAPS THEY'RE CHERRIES OR JAM OR ICING.

4) FRUIT

CUT INTO SMALL PIECES AND PUT ON THE BIRD-TABLE. IF THE BIRDS EAT THEM, THEY'RE SAFE.

Yum-Yum

5) DRINKS OF ALL KINDS

POUR THEM DOWN A PIECE OF WALLPAPER. IF THE WALLPAPER CURLS UP AND FALLS OFF THE WALL THEN YOUR PARENTS WILL BE EXTREMELY ANNOYED AND SEND YOU TO BED WITHOUT ANY SUPPER — WHICH WOULD SOLVE THE PROBLEM OF BEING POISONED!

LABORATORY E
ELECTRONIC FOOD

The scientists at F.R.I.E.D. realize that we live in an electronic age. Laboratory E has been specially set up to experiment with electronic food. Here are some of their reports:

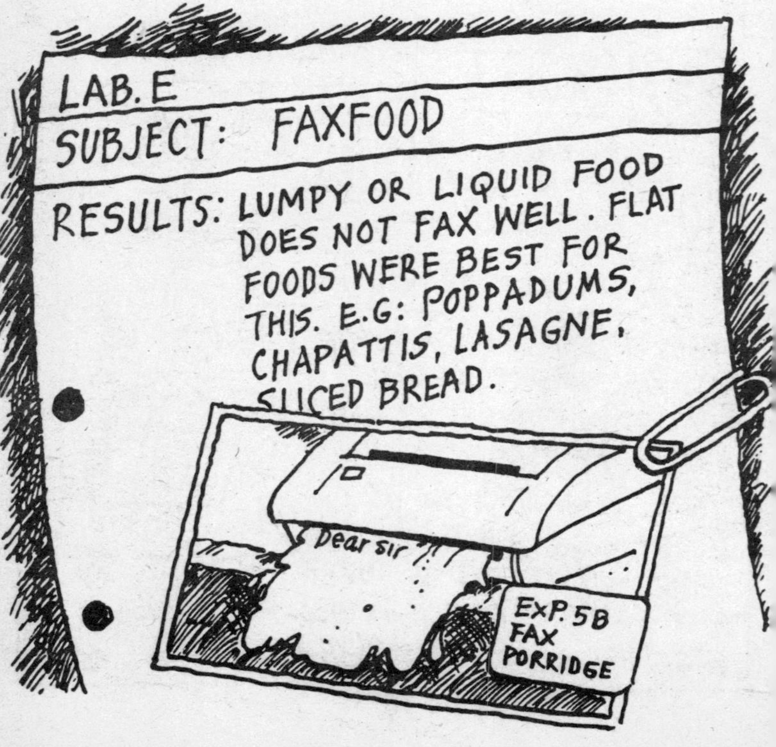

LAB. E

SUBJECT: FAXFOOD

RESULTS: LUMPY OR LIQUID FOOD DOES NOT FAX WELL. FLAT FOODS WERE BEST FOR THIS. E.G: POPPADUMS, CHAPATTIS, LASAGNE, SLICED BREAD.

Dear sir

EXP. 5B
FAX PORRIDGE

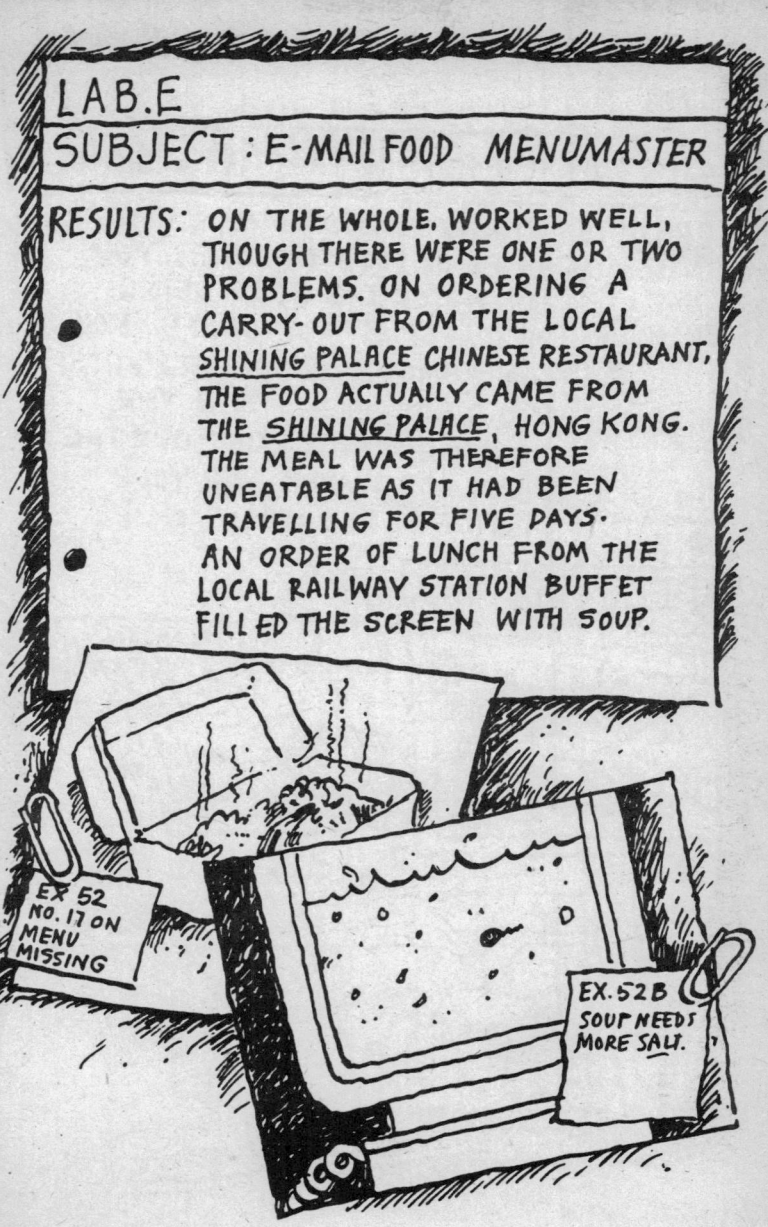

LAB.E
SUBJECT: E-MAIL FOOD MENUMASTER

RESULTS: ON THE WHOLE, WORKED WELL, THOUGH THERE WERE ONE OR TWO PROBLEMS. ON ORDERING A CARRY-OUT FROM THE LOCAL <u>SHINING PALACE</u> CHINESE RESTAURANT, THE FOOD ACTUALLY CAME FROM THE <u>SHINING PALACE</u>, HONG KONG. THE MEAL WAS THEREFORE UNEATABLE AS IT HAD BEEN TRAVELLING FOR FIVE DAYS.
AN ORDER OF LUNCH FROM THE LOCAL RAILWAY STATION BUFFET FILLED THE SCREEN WITH SOUP.

EX 52 NO. 17 ON MENU MISSING

EX. 52B SOUP NEEDS MORE SALT.

LAB. E

SUBJECT: CD-ROM INTERACTIVE COOKING

RESULTS: HIGHLY EDUCATIONAL. THE SHAPE OF FOOD TO COME. YOU CAN WATCH THE FOOD BEING PREPARED BY TOP CHEFS. YOU CAN REMOVE ANY INGREDIENTS YOU DON'T LIKE. THEN THE EQUIPMENT WILL PRINT OUT THE FOOD. ADD WATER AND YOUR DINNER IS SERVED!

BRRRRR!

Exp.91 Food Printout

Exp.91 5min Soak

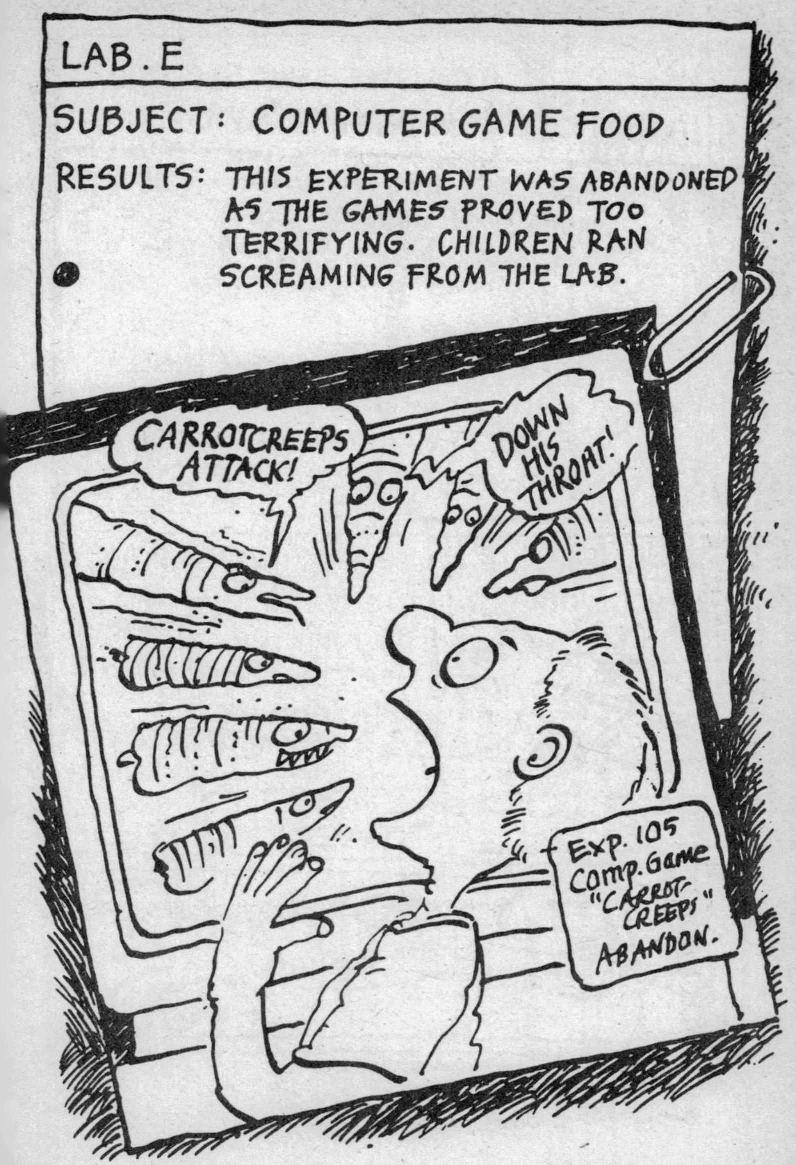

LAB. E

SUBJECT: COMPUTER GAME FOOD

RESULTS: THIS EXPERIMENT WAS ABANDONED AS THE GAMES PROVED TOO TERRIFYING. CHILDREN RAN SCREAMING FROM THE LAB.

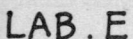

LABORATORIES F1 AND F2..
F.A.S.T. FOOD and F.A.R.T.S. FOOD

We travel round at speed nowadays but can food stand the pace?

VEHICLE	SPEED	WOBBLE GRAPH
SPACE SHUTTLE	MIND-BOGGLINGLY FAST	
INTER-CITY TRAIN	PRETTY FAST	
CAR FERRY	FASTISH	CALM SEA / STORMY SEA
AUNT FREDA'S MINI METRO	SLOW FAST SLOW ETC.	
BIKE	SLOWER THAN ABOVE, JUST	

We have invented a machine called F.A.S.T. - that is, Food At Speed Tester. Some raspberry jellies were put into F.A.S.T. and they were propelled at various speeds to see what would happen.

Test report below:

COMMENTS
SMOOTH RIDE BUT COMPLETE DISINTEGRATION ON LEAVING EARTH'S ATMOSPHERE. SMALL BITS OF JELLY STUCK TO EVERY SURFACE IN THE LAB.
WOBBLED ITSELF INTO A QUIVERING HEAP. WEIGHING IT DOWN WITH AN INTER-CITY BUFFET SANDWICH DIDN'T HELP.
CALM DAY— REMAINED PERFECT. STORMY DAY— DID A CRAZY WALTZ BEFORE FALLING INTO A BUCKET OF WATER (REPRESENTING THE SEA).
WOBBLY AND SLOW TO START WITH, THEN ZOOMED OFF THE F.A.S.T. RAMP AND WAS NEVER SEEN AGAIN (... UNTIL IT WAS FOUND ON THE CEILING A FORTNIGHT LATER).
SMOOTH ROAD — REMAINED UNWOBBLED. MOUNTAIN BIKE TERRAIN — WOBBLED ITSELF INTO AN EXHAUSTED PUDDLE.

Lab. F1 has invented a new range of jellies suitable for travel at speed. The food will survive the journey and you will survive the food.

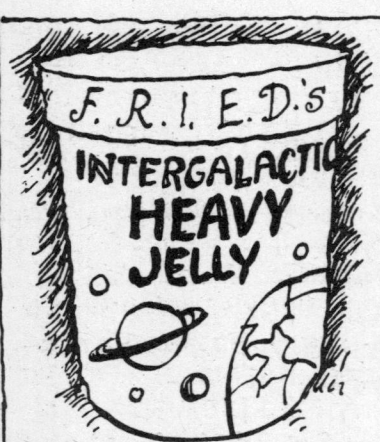

GUARANTEED NOT TO DISINTEGRATE WHEN LEAVING EARTH'S ATMOSPHERE. WEIGHTLESS IN SPACE BUT <u>DO NOT</u> EAT ON EARTH AS YOU WILL PROBABLY FALL THROUGH THE FLOOR.

THESE JELLIES ARE SPHERICAL IN SHAPE. THEY WILL ROLL ABOUT THE TABLE AND FLOOR AND SUFFER LITTLE DAMAGE. EACH PACK INCLUDES A POLISHING CLOTH TO REMOVE DUST, GRIT, ETC.

THESE SEAFARING JELLIES COME WRAPPED IN THEIR OWN LIFE-JACKETS. THIS STOPS THEM ROLLING ABOUT IN A HEAVY SEA. ALSO PREVENTS THEM SINKING IF THEY FALL OVERBOARD.

MADE OF A SPECIAL BOUNCY MIXTURE, THESE JELLIES WILL SURVIVE ALL DRIVING HAZARDS — SUDDEN BRAKING, ACCELERATING, ETC, ETC. DO NOT FEED THEM TO SMALL DOGS AS THEY WILL BOUNCE THEMSELVES OUT OF SIGHT. DO NOT FLICK THEM AT POLICE OFFICERS.

THIS BRILLIANT NEW "SMART FOOD" CHANGES ITSELF TO SUIT THE WOBBLE — IT GROWS MORE SOLID THE MORE IT IS WOBBLED. IT WON'T DISINTEGRATE WHILE ON A BIKE. <u>WARNING</u>: DO NOT JUMP UP AND DOWN WHEN EATING THIS JELLY.

Laboratory F2 is called F.A.R.T.S. meaning Food Acting Restlessly, Thunderously and Stinkily.
Unfortunately, we can't take you in here as the research is top secret. (You wouldn't want to go in anyway.)

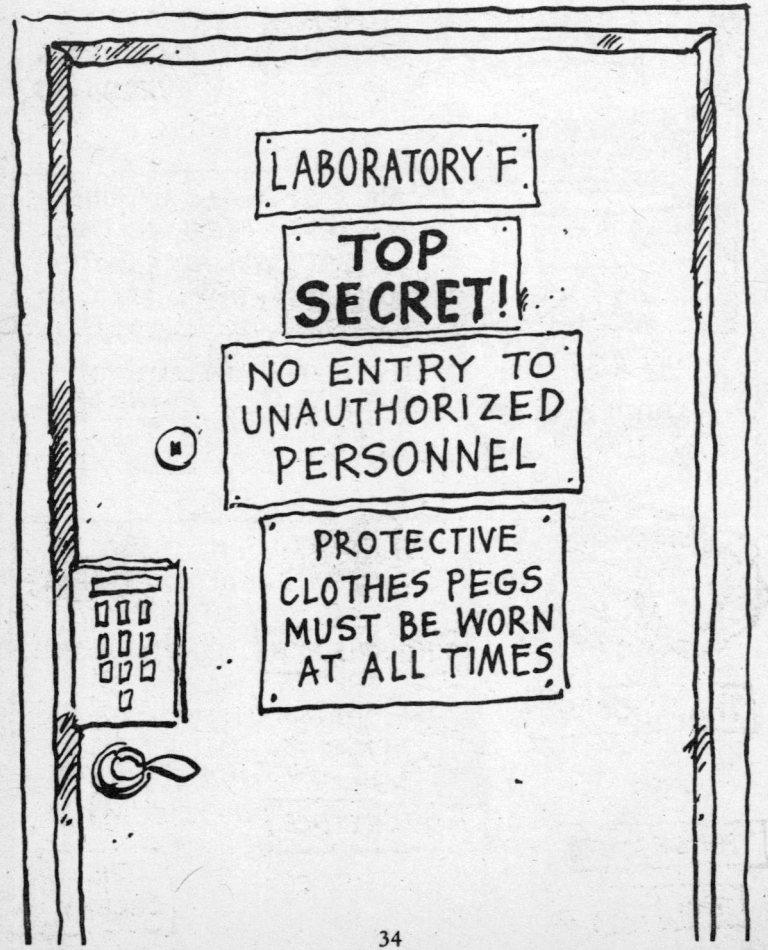

LABORATORY G
GREEN FOOD

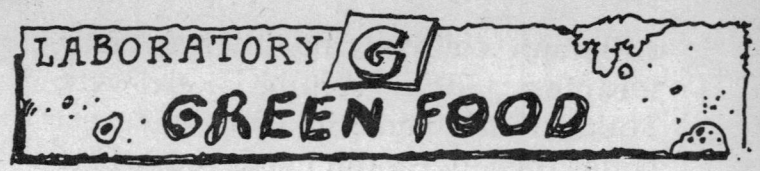

Here is a child getting a very nasty shock:

He has just been given a plateful of dinner made up entirely of GREEN THINGS. For example:

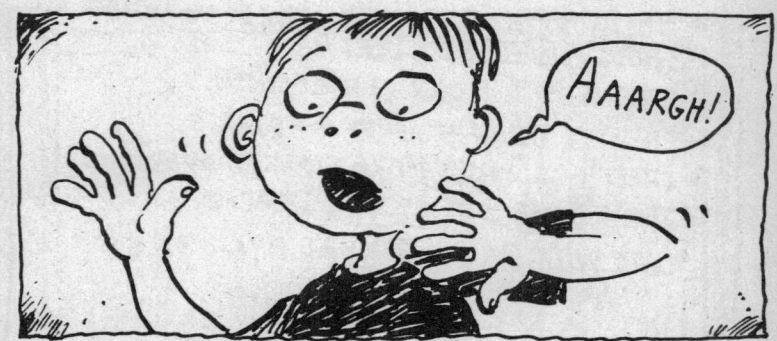

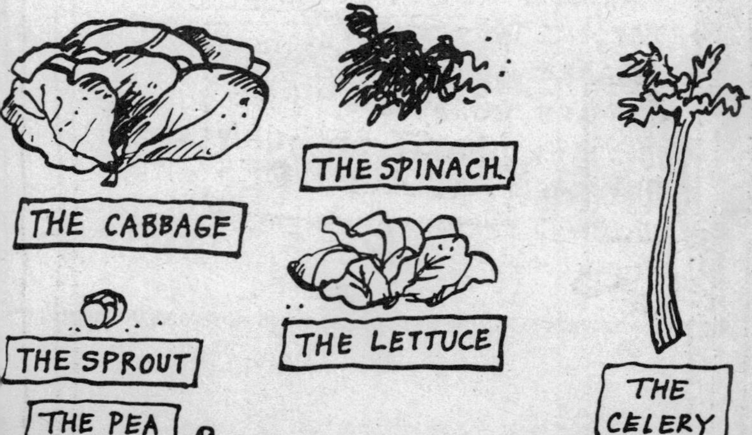

Although children are always being told that GREEN THINGS are very healthy, children keep refusing to eat them. They give millions of excuses. For example:

- WE DON'T EAT ROSEBUSHES SO WHY SHOULD WE EAT CELERY?
- GREEN IS A HORRIBLE COLOUR.
- THEY'VE BEEN SUCKED BY SLUGS.
- CREEPY-CRAWLIES HAVE WALKED OVER THEM.
- THEY COME OUT OF THE GROUND.
- CATS WITH BAD PERSONAL HYGIENE SIT NEAR THEM.
- DOGS HAVE SNIFFED THEM.
- HEDGEHOGS HAVE LICKED THEM. (ALSO RATS, MICE, FOXES, BADGERS, RABBITS, STOATS, WEASELS, TOADS, ELK, ZEBRAS, CAMELS, SNAKES, WARTHOGS ETC., ETC.
- THEY ARE TOO CRUNCHY.
- THEY ARE TOO CHEWY.
- THEY ARE TOO MUSHY.
- THEY FALL/DROP/ROLL OFF THE PLATE.
- THEY SMELL
- COWS AND SHEEP EAT THEM.

In Laboratory G we have solved the problem of surviving GREEN THINGS. We have discovered a tiny bug with the scientific name *Chewus Greenthingius*.

MAGNIFIED A THOUSAND TIMES →

This amazing little bug can eat a million times its own weight in greenery. We will soon be marketing them as small pets. All you need to do is pop them on your dinner plate and the green things will disappear, as if by magic.

However, these bugs will eat *all* green things so you must keep them away from green-coloured curtains, knickers, tooth brushes...

With a little practice you will be able to tell which bug will eat dinner-time green things and which bug will eat other green things.

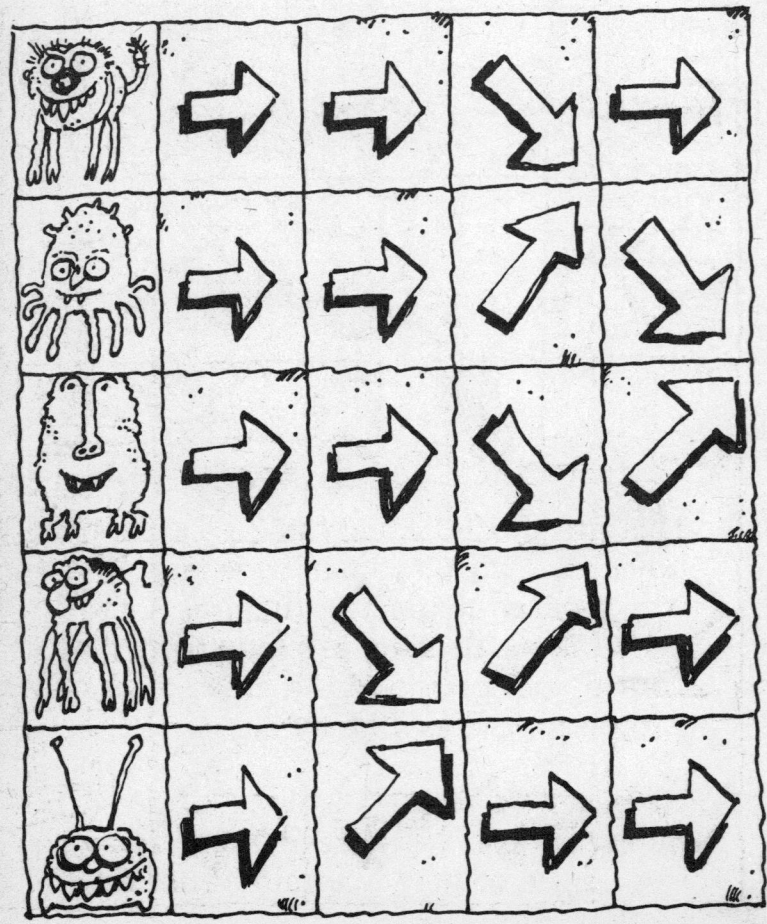

Use the chart below to improve your knowledge of *Chewus Greenthingius*. Choose a bug, then move from square to square, following the arrows, to find the bugs' favourite food.

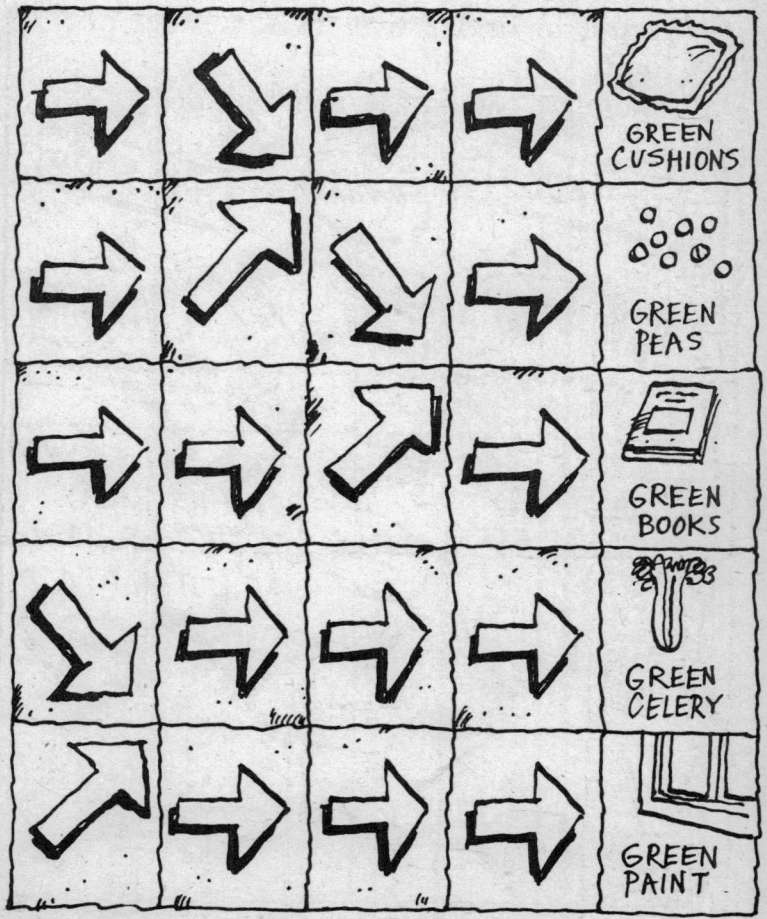

LABORATORY H
HOT FOOD

For many years, Laboratory H has been trying to find a way of surviving hot food.
There are two kinds of hot food:

HOT FOOD *and* HOT FOOD
GLOW GLOW / STEAM STEAM	PULSATE PULSATE
HOWEVER, COLD HOT FOOD OF THIS KIND IS HARMLESS *But*	COLD HOT FOOD OF THIS KIND IS JUST AS HOT AS HOT HOT FOOD.
	PULSATE PULSATE

We hope this makes it clear.

So BEWARE! Hot food can sometimes be H.O.T.T. food, that is, food with a History Of Trauma and Terror.

Another example of H.O.T.T. food happened in 1847 when Amelia Brisket swallowed a whole jar of aniseed balls... but she had lifted a jar of peppercorns from the shelf by mistake.

The result was recorded on the first photograph ever taken.

But the worst H.O.T.T. food is the CHILI. It may be very small but it's DEADLY. Treat it with care.

The most famous H.O.T.T. food is the CURRY. Curries can be mild, hot, very hot, extremely hot, extremely very hot and deadly hot. In Laboratory H we

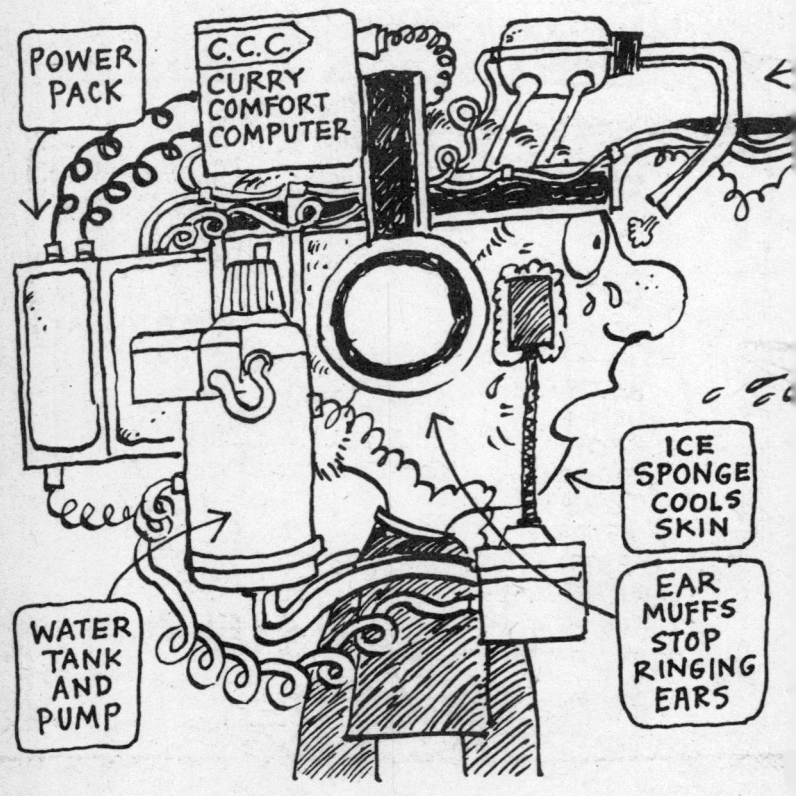

have invented a neat little device to wear when eating curry. It will detect the strength of the curry then cool you down to a comfortable temperature.

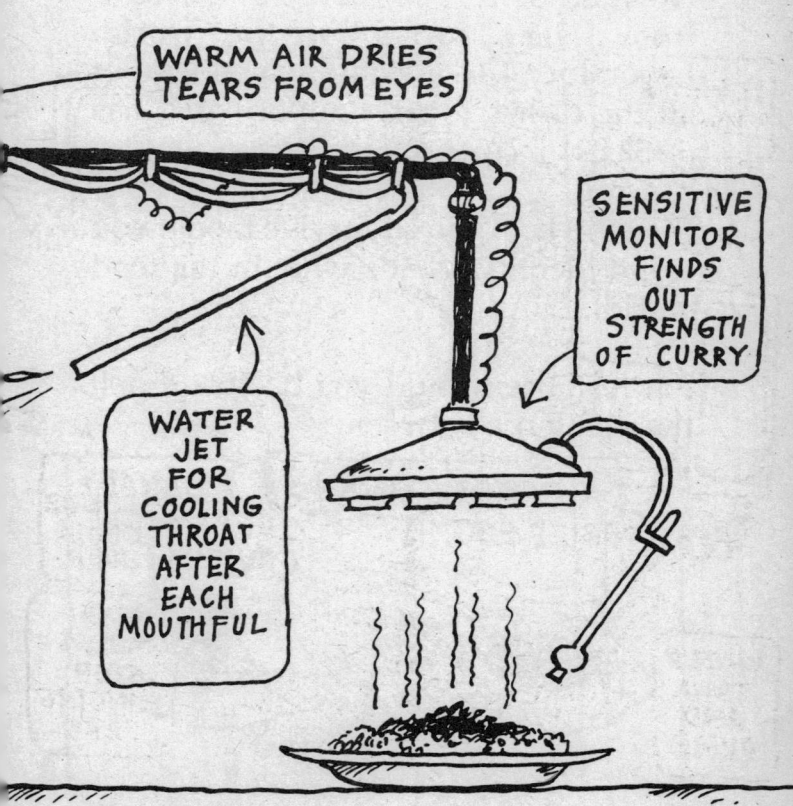

LABORATORY I
IDENTIFYING FOOD

Nowadays, it's possible to eat food from every corner of the world. Laboratory I is making a catalogue of all the dishes it can find. So far it has 6,352,891 recipes.

It would help you to survive food if you could identify what's what in the food world.

For instance, would you be able to tell the difference between:

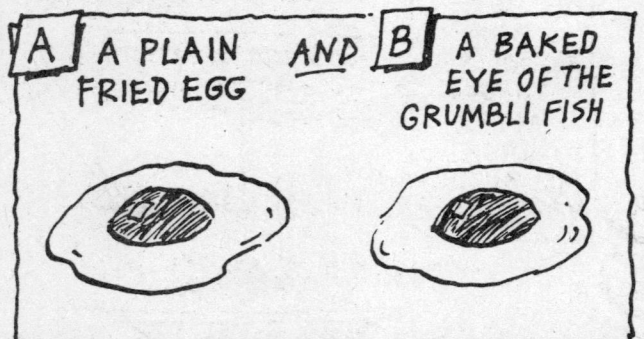

Try the following little test which will sharpen up your international food knowledge.
(Answers on page 49).

IS THIS:

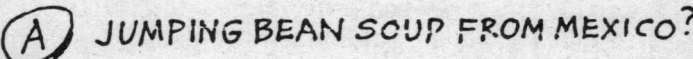

(A) JUMPING BEAN SOUP FROM MEXICO?

(B) A DISH OF SIBERIAN CAT FOOD?

(C) EXPLODING RICE FROM MADAGASCAR?

IS THIS:

(A) VAMPIRE PIE FROM VENEZUELA?

(B) JELLY CAKE FROM AUSTRIA?

(C) A RHUBARB TART WOBBLING ITSELF TO DEATH ON A TRAIN? (SEE FAST FOOD).

3

IS THIS:

- **A** VOLCANIC STEW FROM JAPAN?
- **B** SOMETHING THAT'S BEEN IN A HUNGARIAN OVEN TOO LONG?
- **C** ROAST COTTON-WOOL PLANT FROM ZAMBIA?

4

IS THIS:

- **A** MACTAVISH'S WILD HAGGIS FROM SCOTLAND?
- **B** ROAST WELSH RUGBY BALL?
- **C** STIR-FRY ARMADILLO FROM ARGENTINA?

ANSWERS

1. B THIS IS A DISH OF SIBERIAN CAT FOOD. FLEAS CROUCH ON THE CAT FOOD UNTIL THE CAT COMES. THEY LEAP OUT OF THE WAY SO THEY DON'T GET EATEN, THEN LEAP BACK ON TO THE CAT'S NOSE.

2. A VAMPIRE PIE IS THE SAME AS BLACKBIRD PIE. WHEN VENEZUELANS THROW A PARTY THEY SING THIS SONG.
SING A SONG OF SIXPENCE,
A POCKET FULL OF RYE,
FOUR-AND-TWENTY VAMPIRES
BAKED IN A PIE...
WHEN THE PIE IS OPENED THE VAMPIRES FLY OUT AND BITE THE PARTY GUESTS.

3. A VOLCANIC STEW TAKES ABOUT A FORTNIGHT TO COOL DOWN. JAPANESE MEALS LIKE THIS LAST A LONG, LONG TIME.

4. C ARMADILLOS HAVE A VERY TOUGH SKIN AND ROLL THEMSELVES INTO A BALL WHEN THREATENED. SO ARMADILLOS USUALLY GET UP AND WALK AWAY AFTER BEING STIR-FRIED. THAT JUST LEAVES THE VEGETABLES WITH A DELICIOUS TANG OF DILLO.

The joke-food laboratory at F.R.I.E.D. has invented many famous funny foods. For instance:
- Fireworks that explode in popcorn instead of sparks.
- Novelty-filled cushions. For example, cushions filled with porridge, hard-boiled eggs or crisps.
- Chips with micro chips which hop about when you turn on the radio.

If you're feeling bored with food then a quick look through Laboratory J's book – *1001 FOOD JOKES* – will help you survive.

Knock knock!
Who's there?
Butter
Butter Who?
Butter be quick, I have to go to the loo!

Knock knock!
Who's there?
Pudding.
Pudding who?
Pudding on your shoes before your trousers is a bad idea!

Knock knock!
Who's there?
Roland.
Roland who?
Roland butter, please!

Knock knock!
Who's there?
Candy.
Candy who?
Candy cow jump over the moon?

Knock knock!
Who's there?
Eggs.
Eggs who?
Eggstremely cold waiting for you to open the door!

Knock knock!
Who's there?
Maida.
Maida who?
Maida cake 'cos I knew you were coming.

Knock knock!
Who's there?
Tuna.
Tuna who?
Tuna violin and it will sound better!

Knock knock!
Who's there?
Cereal.
Cereal who?
Cereal pleasure to meet you!

LABORATORY K — THE KITCHEN

The kitchen is where your food is stored and prepared.
The kitchen can be a frightening place. Here are a few hazards you must look out for when you're in search of food.

CUPBOARDS AND SURFACES

PART 1

THE INCREDIBLY CLEAN KITCHEN. THE ROOM LOOKS LIKE AN OPERATING THEATRE OR A DESERT. YOU MUST BE VERY CAREFUL NOT TO PUT ANYTHING ON THE SHINING SURFACES. (E.G. FOOTBALL BOOTS, JAM, BREATH ETC.) ON NO ACCOUNT TAKE YOUR FRIENDS IN THERE TO SHARE A PACKET OF BISCUITS. YOU WILL DIE OF STARVATION ADMIRING THE NEAT CUPBOARDS AND CONTAINERS.

CUPBOARDS AND SURFACES

PART 2

THE INCREDIBLY UNTIDY KITCHEN. YOU WILL FIND THERE'S NOWHERE TO LAY ANYTHING HERE. YOU MAY DIE OF STARVATION TRYING TO FIND THE BREAD. YOU MAY BE BADLY INJURED IN AN AVALANCHE WHEN YOU OPEN A CUPBOARD

FRIDGES

MILK IS ONE OF THOSE THINGS THAT WILL CHANGE AS YOU LOOK AT IT. IT WILL TURN FROM WHITE AND FRESH TO GREEN AND CHEESY IN THE BLINK OF AN EYE. FRIDGES ARE USUALLY FULL OF THESE LURKING MONSTERS.

FOOD

FOOD ALWAYS SEEMS TO GET ON OTHER FOOD. YOU'LL FIND TOAST ON THE BUTTER, BUTTER ON THE JAM, JAM ON THE CHEESE, COFFEE IN THE SUGAR, ETC. JUST REMEMBER IT'S ALL GOING TO END UP IN THE SAME PLACE.

PETS: THE DOG

WHEREVER YOU TURN IN THE KITCHEN YOU WILL FIND THE DOG. THE DOG HAS A PERMANENT "FEED ME" EXPRESSION ON ITS FACE. THE DOG IS ALWAYS IN YOUR WAY. FEED A DOG A CHOCOLATE BISCUIT AND IT WILL WANT ANOTHER. DON'T FEED THE DOG AND IT WILL START LICKING THE KITCHEN. YOU CAN'T WIN.

PETS: THE CAT

UNFORTUNATELY FOR THE DOG, THE CUPBOARDS IT CAN REACH ARE USUALLY FULL OF PANS OR SOAP POWDER. CATS CAN REACH HIGHER AND RAID THE CUPBOARDS FULL OF BISCUITS AND JAM. CHECK HIGH CUPBOARDS REGULARLY FOR FAT CATS.

Laboratory K has been making a study of kitchens and how to survive them. Just how hazardous is *your* kitchen? Try the Lab. K hazard test.

1 HAS YOUR CAT DISCOVERED HOW TO USE THE CAN-OPENER?

(YES) — 100 POINTS   (NO) — 1 POINT

2 HAS YOUR CAT USED ANY OF THE FOLLOWING ON THE DOG?

- A A LEMON SQUEEZER — 1 POINT
- B A BLENDER — 6 POINTS
- C A NUT-CRACKER — 50 POINTS

3 HAVE YOU EVER FOUND MICE IN THE MICROWAVE?

(YES) — 20 POINTS   (NO, ONLY A RAT) — 30 POINTS

4 HAVE YOU EVER FOUND ANY OF THE FOLLOWING IN THE WASHING MACHINE?

- A CLOTHES — 2 POINTS
- B CUTLERY — 5 POINTS
- C THE CAT (HAVING A SHOWER) — 10 POINTS
- D A DECOMPOSING COD — 20 POINTS
- E A LIVE COD — 50 POINTS

5 HAVE YOU SEEN ANY OF THE FOLLOWING RUN ACROSS THE KITCHEN?

- A A COCKROACH — 3 POINTS
- B A SNAKE — 10 POINTS
- C A PIECE OF CHEESE — 93 POINTS

6 WHEN YOU OPEN YOUR OVEN DOOR DO YOU HEAR:

- A THE CRACKLING OF BURNT STICKY THINGS ROUND THE DOOR-EDGE? — 10 POINTS
- B WEIRD CACKLING LAUGHTER FROM THE DARK BIT AT THE VERY BACK? — 1,000 POINTS

7 HAS ANY CAN OR BOTTLE IN YOUR KITCHEN EXPLODED AND KNOCKED OUT:

- A THE DOG? — 3 POINTS
- B THE POSTMAN? — 10 POINTS
- C THE NEIGHBOUR THREE DOORS ALONG? — 50 POINTS
- D SOMEONE ON THE OTHER SIDE OF THE COUNTRY — 1,567 POINTS

TOT UP YOUR SCORE. ANYTHING OVER 10 POINTS MEANS THAT YOUR KITCHEN IS A HAZARD ZONE — EAT OUT!

LABORATORY L LUNCHBOX FOOD

What do you like to find in your school lunch box? Laboratory L's research has revealed some interesting things. Here are a few examples:

KEVIN SPROUT

His lunch box contained:
- A rolled-up comic
- His pet hamster
- Six marbles
- A Gameboy
- A crisp

AMANDA GHERKINO

Her lunch box contained:
- A fluffy toy covered in marmalade
- A cheese roll covered in fluff
- A chocolate biscuit smeared with cheese
- Everything smeared in yogurt

AUGUSTUS EGGE

His lunch box contained:
- A packet of sandwiches used as a cushion (flat)
- A packet of crisps used as a football (dust)
- An apple used as a cricket ball (juice)

JAMES McJAMS

His lunch box contained:
- Yesterday's banana
- Last week's biscuit
- Last month's sandwich
- Last year's green mould

TINA PEARS

Her lunch box contained:
- Three pairs of scissors
- A packet of cotton wool
- A corn parer
- Various plasters
- Various ointments

(She had picked up her mother's chiropodist's case)

Surviving the things in your lunch box can be quite difficult. They can sometimes be very boring or very old.

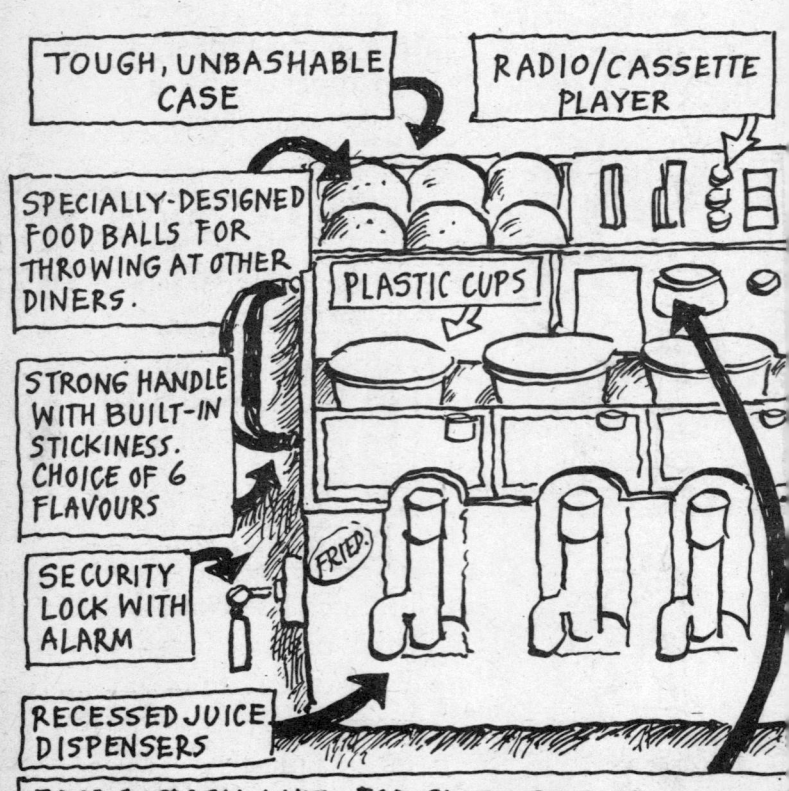

Laboratory L has invented a new, luxury lunch box which will make lunch time at school an exciting and comforting experience.

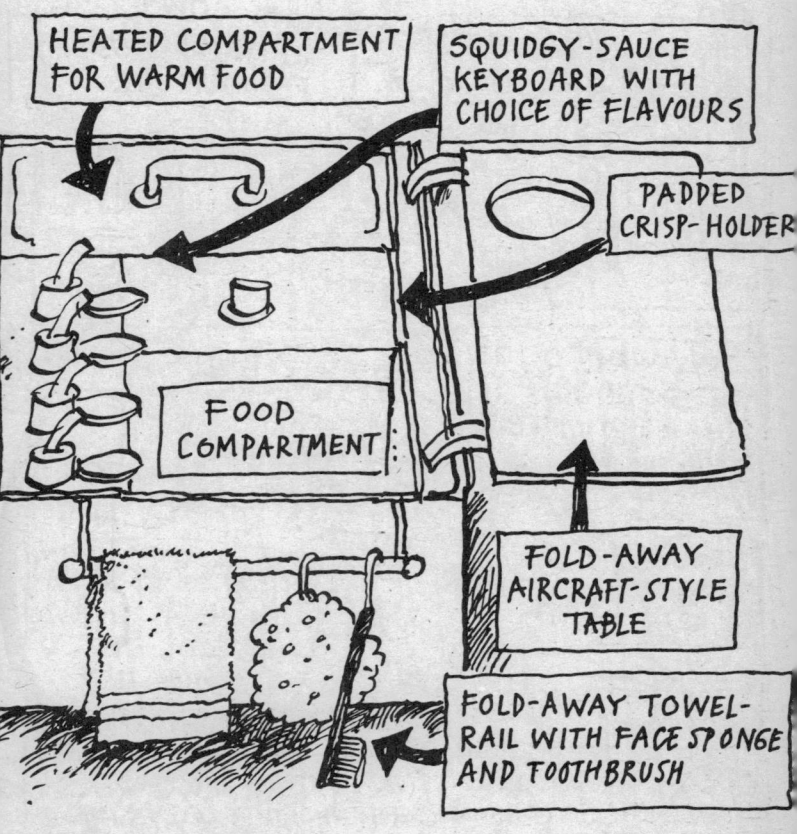

LABORATORY M: MISSILE FOOD

It's difficult enough to survive food slipping down your throat - it's even worse surviving a piece of food thrown across the school dining-hall or dropped from a passing aeroplane.

Laboratory M has been studying the effects of missile food. Look at the diagrams below and prepare yourself for airborne nosh.

EGGS, SOFT TOMATOES	CUCUMBERS, BANANAS
THE TRADITIONAL FOOD FOR PELTING PEOPLE WITH. MESSY AND COLOURFUL YET HARMLESS.	FLY THROUGH THE AIR WITH A SPINNING MOTION. DIFFICULT TO AIM BUT DEADLY. SOME CURVED BANANAS MAY HAVE A BOOMERANG EFFECT.

GRAPES, PEANUTS	**CUSTARD PIES, DISHES WITH MINCE, RICE OR SAUCE**
Usually thrown by small children. Harmless and fun. Can be caught in the mouth with practice.	Really messy and embarrassing. Gooey and slippery. Ruin clothes.

HARD APPLES, PINEAPPLES, COCONUTS	**SPECIALLY-DESIGNED FOOD BALLS (SEE PAGE 62)**
The most deadly missile food. Dodge it if you can. Always keep an eye on the sky for food falling from hot air balloons.	Lab K's harmless food balls are squidgy, sticky and smell foody. Harmless food-throwing!

 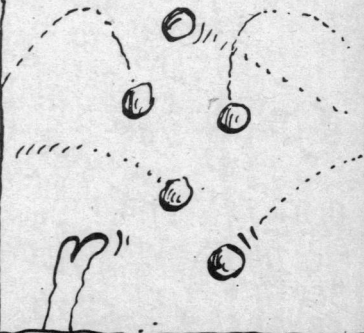

LABORATORY N
NIGHT FOOD

Everyone, at some time or another, has had a bout of night starvation. But what kind of food is best to eat in bed? Let's lift the covers of one of Laboratory N's many beds and see how you can survive a midnight feast.

SANDWICHES: THE TWO HALVES OFTEN GET SEPARATED FROM THE MIDDLE.

ORANGES AND APPLES: GOOD BED FOOD, EASY TO STORE BUT PEEL AND CORE A NUISANCE. CAN ROLL OFF THE BED AND THUMP ON THE FLOOR.

SALADS: GO LIMP AND CLAMMY LIKE HAVING A REPTILE UNDER THE SHEETS.

BISCUITS: FILL THE BED WITH CRUMBS.

CRISPS: LIKE BISCUITS ONLY SHARPER.

ICE CREAM AND ICE LOLLIES:
NOT VERY GOOD IF YOU HAVE A HOT-WATER BOTTLE OR ELECTRIC BLANKET. WILL QUICKLY BECOME A PUDDLE.

CHOCOLATE:
MELTS AND LEAVES NASTY BROWN STAINS ON THE COVERS.

ITALIAN SAUSAGE:
EXCELLENT BED FOOD. CAN BE KEPT AT THE FOOT OF THE BED OR UNDER THE PILLOW FOR WEEKS.

NOODLES:
VERY HANDY! BUT IF THEY ESCAPE TURN INTO SLIMY MAGGOTS ESPECIALLY BETWEEN THE TOES.

THE CAT AND THE DOG:
KEEP AN EYE ON THESE ANIMALS. YOU MAY FIND THEM IN YOUR BED HOOVERING UP THE CRUMBS OR MUNCHING THROUGH YOUR EMERGENCY NIGHT-TIME STORE CUPBOARD.

LABORATORY O
ODOROUS FOOD

Laboratory O specializes in odorous food – in other words, niffy nosh. We can smell what we are going to eat long before the food reaches our mouths.

| THERE ARE DELICIOUS SMELLS LIKE FRESHLY BAKED BREAD... | ...AND THERE ARE NOT SO DELICIOUS SMELLS LIKE ROTTEN CHEESE. |

Lab. O has been testing the odours of many foods. Can you survive the odour test? Read the smelly descriptions opposite and choose which dish you would most like to eat. Then turn over the page and find out what delicacy you have chosen.

A HOT SPICY SMELL. SLIGHTLY OILY. A HINT OF BURNING RUBBER AND PETROL FUMES.

AN EXOTIC SMELL OF GARLIC, ONIONS AND A TOUCH OF VINEGAR. ALSO A WHIFF OF STALE ARMPITS AND CARROTS.

UNMISTAKABLE FISHY AND CHIPPY SMELL, BUT WITH THE ADDITION OF SINGED FLUFF AND THE TANG OF SOUR WATER.

THE SMELL OF ROSE BLOSSOM, VIOLETS AND DISINFECTANT ADDED TO THE SCENT OF FRESH STRAWBERRIES.

A TASTY MEAT AND CHUTNEY SMELL BUT ALSO A HINT OF COD AND WELLY BOOT.

A CURRY CARRY-OUT FROM THE *INDIA PALACE* RESTAURANT BROUGHT TO YOU BY EXPRESS BIKE DELIVERY SERVICE. (FELL OFF AT THE TRAFFIC LIGHTS.) (TWICE.)

ROAST PICKLED SLOTH WITH CARROT PURÉE

FISH AND CHIPS FROM ERNIE'S. HE THOUGHT THE CAT FELL INTO THE DEEP FAT FRIER. HE TRIED TO FISH IT OUT WITH A MOP, BUT THE MOP-HEAD FELL IN, TOO.

STRAWBERRY TART WITH A SAUCE MADE FROM EVERYTHING ON THE BATHROOM SHELF.

A SANDWICH THAT FELL OFF A CHANNEL FERRY AND LANDED ON A FISHING BOAT

LABORATORY P
PARTY FOOD

Party food is usually special, brightly-coloured and scrumptious. The thing you have to worry about is how to survive the other party guests and get as much party food as you can. Follow Laboratory P's Five-point Party Food Survival Plan for complete success.

1) PARTY TABLE EYEBALLING

WHEN YOU ARRIVE AT THE PARTY, HAVE A GOOD LOOK AT THE FOOD ON THE TABLE. TRY TO MEMORIZE THE LAYOUT AND WHERE ALL YOUR FAVOURITE FOODS ARE.

2) PARTY REMNANTS COLLECTION

COLLECT UP BITS OF PARTY STUFF LIKE STREAMERS, BURST BALLOONS (REALLY EFFECTIVE) AND SCRAPS OF WRAPPING PAPER. SLIP THEM INTO SANDWICHES THAT OTHER PEOPLE ARE GOING TO EAT. THIS WILL SLOW THEIR EATING DOWN OR EVEN PUT PEOPLE OFF.

3) PARTY CLOTHES STAIN TECHNIQUE

ICE CREAM IS WONDERFULLY SLOPPY. "ACCIDENTALLY" SLOPPING STRAWBERRY AND CHOCOLATE ICE CREAM DOWN OTHER GUESTS' CLOTHES WILL SEND THEM OFF WHINING AND LOOKING FOR A WET CLOTH. DON'T SLOP ANYMORE THAN THREE TIMES OR ADULTS GET SUSPICIOUS.

4) JELLY-SLOBBER

JELLY CAN BE USED IN THE SAME WAY AS ICE CREAM. IT'S BEST DROPPED DOWN <u>INSIDE</u> CLOTHES. TRIFLE CAN BE USED TOO, BUT THIS IS <u>VERY</u> DARING.

5) DISTRACT AND NUDGE

IF YOU'VE WORKED QUICKLY, YOU WILL HAVE GOT RID OF ABOUT HALF THE GUESTS. HERE'S THE FINAL TRICK (NEEDS PRACTICE) — WHEN THE ADULT CUTS THE BIRTHDAY CAKE, DISTRACT ATTENTION BY POINTING ACROSS THE ROOM AND — NUDGE THE KNIFE SO YOU GET A BIGGER PORTION OF CAKE.

NUDGE QUICKLY AND GENTLY

LABORATORY Q
QUIRKY FOOD

'One man's meat is another man's poison' goes the old saying.
For example:

WHY DO WE EAGERLY TUCK INTO A PRAWN COCKTAIL (LITTLE, PALE-COLOURED WRIGGLY THINGS FROM THE SEA)...

BUT

WE LOOK WITH HORROR AT A NATIVE SOUTH AMERICAN TUCKING INTO A PLATEFUL OF GRUBS (LITTLE, PALE-COLOURED WRIGGLY THINGS FROM THE LAND)?

Laboratory Q studies quirky food from all over the world. They may be able to give us some answers as to why...

...the French bake loaves that are dangerous weapons.

...the Italians make pasta that tangles itself into a huge knot.

...people in the East eat with two sticks. ...and why people in the West eat with four little sticks on the end of a stick.

All these queries, and more, could be explained by the scientists in Lab. Q. Unfortunately, they're all away finding out why the inhabitants of Patagonia roll penguin eggs wrapped in spinach down the sides of high mountains.

LABORATORY R
RECORD-BREAKING FOOD

The scientists in Laboratory R spend their time weighing and measuring food. All the information is stored in their huge computer and now and again they come up with some fascinating facts. Here are one or two facts about record-breaking food.

THE BOUNCIEST LUMP OF PORRIDGE WAS DISCOVERED BOUNCING THROUGH LIVERPOOL LAST MONTH. EXPERTS SAID THAT, JUDGING BY ITS SHAPE, IT HAD BEEN BOUNCING FOR AT LEAST SIX MONTHS. IT HAD PROBABLY BOUNCED ALL THE WAY FROM ORKNEY.

THE LARGEST CHAPATTI EVER BAKED MEASURED ABOUT 27 METRES IN DIAMETER. IT WAS USED FOR A WHOLE SEASON AS A TENNIS COURT COVER.

AN ALLOTMENT OWNER, BERT STRINGY, CAME ACROSS A POTATO WHICH WAS MAKING A STRANGE NOISE. HE SENT IT TO LAB.R AT F.R.I.E.D. MANY TESTS WERE CARRIED OUT AND IT WAS DISCOVERED IT COULD HUM A TOTAL OF SIX TUNES.

All this may seem a load of pointless information. But remember, Laboratory R is interested in *any* unusual foods. This may help you survive food which you don't want to eat.

Amanda, finish your meal!

I can't. I want to send it to F.R.I.E.D. The cabbage is the limpest cabbage in the world. The smell has just killed two flies stone-dead and the sausages have done twenty press-ups each.

LABORATORY S
SECRET FOOD

Laboratory S specializes in finding places to hide food - either food you don't want but you've been told to eat, or food you want to eat but have been told you can't have.

Here's Lab. S's survival guide to secret food:

ALWAYS REMEMBER WHERE YOU PUT FOOD, ESPECIALLY IF IT IS SOMETHING THAT WILL GO OFF. A PONGY SMELL COMING FROM BEHIND THE WARDROBE IS A DEAD GIVE-AWAY.

SMALL, LIGHT ITEMS CAN BE HIDDEN BEHIND PAINTINGS OR WALL-MIRRORS.

FOR QUICK BUT TEMPORARY HIDING - A PACKET OF BISCUITS CAN BE SLIPPED INTO THE VIDEO.

SLIP FOOD UNDERNEATH.

THE WEIGHT OF THE PAINTING WILL HOLD FOOD IN PLACE.

BUT DON'T FORGET IT OR YOU MAY GET A VERY STRANGE PICTURE NEXT TIME YOU SWITCH ON THE TELEVISION.

DON'T HIDE THINGS WHERE JUICE OR GRAVY MIGHT RUN DOWN THE WALLPAPER OR WHERE PARENTS MIGHT SNOOP, LIKE SOCK DRAWERS OR SCHOOL BAGS.

PACKETS OF FOOD AND CANS CAN BE HIDDEN BETWEEN BOOKS ON A SHELF OR IN AMONG OLD TOYS.

IF YOU HAVE A DOG, MAKE SURE IT'S IN ATTENDANCE WHEN YOU'RE EATING SOMETHING CRUMBLY. IT WILL DESTROY THE EVIDENCE BY LICKING UP THE CRUMBS.

NOTE: ALWAYS GET YOUR DOG TO WEAR DARK GLASSES OTHERWISE THE GUILTY 'I'VE-BEEN-GIVEN-A-TITBIT' LOOK IN ITS EYES WILL MAKE ADULTS SUSPICIOUS.

IN FACT, DOGS AND CATS ARE IDEAL FOR GETTING RID OF FOOD YOU DON'T WANT — BUT COMPARE WITH PAGES 57, 69 AND 85.

LABORATORY T
TUMMY-GURGLING FOOD

Tummy gurgling is a great embarrassment and food is the cause of it. It's very difficult to control but Lab. T's helpful chart will enable you to identify the gurgle and try to hide it.

SOUND	TYPE	ACTION
BLIRP... BLURP	MINOR GURGLE	WILL NOT BE HEARD ABOVE SURROUNDING NOISE. TAKE NO ACTION.
BLURP... BLIMP... BLURRR...	MEDIUM GURGLE	CAN BE MASKED BY COUGHING OR BY TALKING A LITTLE LOUDER.
BLUUURRR RRR....	EXTENDED GURGLE	CAN BE QUITE EMBARRASSING. A BURST OF SINGING IS THE ONLY ANSWER.
BRUMBLOOP... NRRLOOOMP!	A RUMBLE	A VERY LOUD SHRIEK OF LAUGHTER IS NEEDED HERE.
BRUMMM... BDOOMF!!	VOLCANIC ERUPTION	QUICKLY LEAVE THE HOUSE, TRAIN, PLANE OR WHEREVER YOU HAPPEN TO BE.

LABORATORY U
USEFUL FOOD

Laboratory U is the place where other uses are found for food you don't want. Here are some of their headline-grabbers. You might get some ideas!

SCIENTISTS CREATE DRY SKI-SLOPE FROM BANANA SKINS

"IT'S A WINNER!" SAYS OLYMPIC SKIER PAM SNOSLOPE-WILKINS.

BUSINESS NEWS

COMPANY RIDING HIGH ON SPORTS SHOE PROFITS

A NEW TYPE OF SOLE MADE FROM HEAT-TREATED BLANCMANGE WHICH WILL ALLOW ATHLETES TO CLIMB WALLS IS SET TO CHANGE THE FACE OF COMPETITIVE SPORT.

LABORATORY V
VANISHING FOOD

Unfortunately, Lab V has vanished..
Favourite food often has a habit of vanishing. Boxes of chocolates suffer most from this. All the *best* chocolates mysteriously disappear, leaving the nasty, dry tasteless ones.

No matter how closely you keep an eye on family and friends, you will never catch the culprit.

Dogs and cats can also make food vanish but you'll know when they're to blame because they will have guilt written all over their faces.

(See also dogs and cats, Lab. K and dogs and cats, Lab. S).

LABORATORY W
WEATHER FORECASTING with FOOD

It is a very little-known fact that food is excellent for forecasting the weather. Laboratory W gives a weather forecast twice a day using the following methods:

THE SAUSAGE RAIN GAUGE

IN VERY DRY WEATHER THE SAUSAGE ON THE STRING BECOMES THIN AND WRINKLY. WHEN RAIN IS ON THE WAY THE SAUSAGE BECOMES PLUMP AND SHINY.

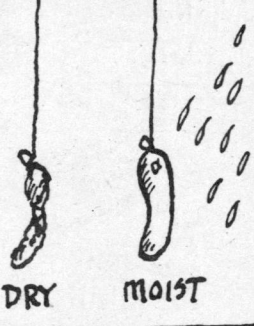

DRY   MOIST

THE LEMONADE WIND STRENGTH GAUGE

CALM   BREEZY   HURRICANE!

ON CALM DAYS THE BOTTLE OF LEMONADE DOESN'T MOVE. ON WINDY DAYS IT WILL SWAY FROM SIDE TO SIDE. DURING A HURRICANE THE BOTTLE DANCES ABOUT SO MUCH THAT THE FIZZ BLOWS THE CAP OFF.

THE LETTUCE TEMPERATURE GAUGE

THE LETTUCE WILL LOOK FRESH AND STAND UPRIGHT ON COOL DAYS. IT WILL BECOME FLABBY ON HOT DAYS AND WILL TURN BLACK IN A FROST.

COOL

HOT

VERY COLD

THE LEEK WEATHER-VANE

THE FLAPPING LEAVES OF THE LEEK WILL TELL YOU WHICH DIRECTION THE WIND IS COMING FROM.

ROLL RAIN GAUGE

THE AMOUNT OF RAIN WHICH HAS FALLEN CAN BE MEASURED WITH THE ROLL GAUGE. LAY A TRAY OF SIX ROLLS OUT IN A DOWNPOUR THEN SQUEEZE THEM OUT INTO A SPECIAL MEASURING JUG.

SEVERE WEATHER TESTS

THROW AN APPLE INTO THE GARDEN FROM AN UPSTAIRS WINDOW. IF IT BOUNCES, THE WEATHER IS DRY. IF IT GOES SPLAT, THERE HAS BEEN A LOT OF RAIN. IF IT BOBS OFF OUT OF SIGHT — FLOOD WARNING!

THE HAIL GAUGE

PLACE A CAN OF BAKED BEANS IN THE MIDDLE OF A LAWN OR DRIVEWAY. HAIL WILL RATTLE NOISILY ON THE CAN TOP.

LINK SAUSAGE SNOW GAUGE

A VERY HANDY WAY TO TELL JUST HOW DEEP THE SNOW IS. IF YOU CAN'T SEE ANY SAUSAGE AT ALL, THEN GET OUT THOSE SPADES!

LABORATORY X
X-RATED FOOD

For those of you who like to dice with death, Laboratory X is the place for you. The researchers in Lab. X have put together the *Menu From Hell* - not for faint-hearted diners. If you survive this, you'll survive anything.

Menu ~ First Course

FISH SOUP FROM THE OCEAN DEPTHS

Trawling the deepest, darkest parts of the Atlantic, six of the ugliest fish ever seen have been used to make this delicious soup. Created by master chef Antonio di Icer.

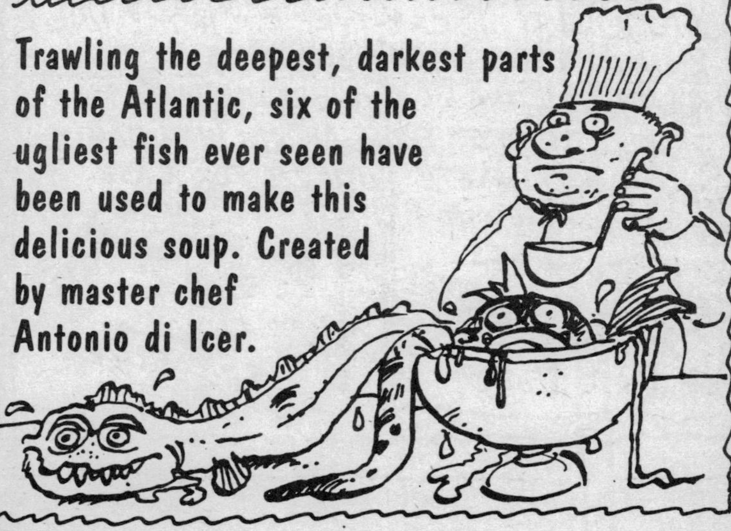

Menu ~ Main Course

MRS SCROTCHIT'S STEAK AND KIDNEY PIE

Mrs Scrotchit is the landlady of the Motorwayview Boarding House. She's been serving the same steak and kidney pie for the last forty years - yes, the *same*, one and only steak pie. It's so awful that none of her guests can eat it, so she puts the ingredients away each day after meal-times for re-use the next time - very economical!

STEAK: BITS OF CAR-TYRE CUT INTO CHUNKS.
KIDNEY: TABLE-TENNIS BALLS.
GRAVY: ENGINE OIL AND BROWN VARNISH
PASTRY: LEATHER FROM AN OLD HANDBAG (COMPLETE WITH ZIP FOR EASY ACCESS TO FILLING).

Menu ~ Pudding

DINNER-LADY DESSERT

Brought to you by the head dinner-lady, Cowpatt Primary School.

Her speciality is the Heavy-Rock Steam Pudding. The pudding is so heavy that the head dinner-lady has to pump iron daily to build up muscles strong enough to lift it.

School children who have eaten even the finiest slice of the pudding have been unable to get up off the floor for four hours.

LABORATORY Y YOUNGSTER FOOD

Are you one of those people who finds eating a complete bore?

Does moving your jaws up and down and backwards and forwards for twenty minutes tire you out?

The kitchens of Laboratory Y have come up with the answer to how to survive food – Youngster Food.

- It is very similar to the little jars of mushy stuff you give babies but much more exciting.
- It is easy to eat - you can even suck it through a straw. For those of you too busy to stop and eat, we provide a special holster for the jars.

Mind you, all the food looks much the same.

Some of you may find this a bit dull, therefore Laboratory Y can provide an addition to the holster – a picture-holder into which you can slip an appetizing photograph of the food you are eating (or sucking).

There is also a tape and tape-player available. The tape contains half-an-hour of foody noises – crunching lettuce, crackling packets, munching biscuits and other such delicious sounds.

All this will provide the feel of genuine eating but with no effort at all.

LABORATORY Z
ZOMBIE FOOD

Do you eat the Zombie or does the Zombie eat you...?